Mouse Town Notice Board

Announcement:

The Great Car Race

Date; Mouse Day

Place; Starting line is in front of
the Mouse Assembly Hall

Grand Prize: The Ultimate Piece of Cheese
(It´s the biggest cheese anyone
has ever seen!)

Bon Bon with his yellow scarf is easy going and very strong. He enjoys collecting things.

Whisk has a funny little knot in his tail. He's a very clever mechanic and inventor.

Teeny, the youngest, is never without her green bracelet. She is very loyal and doesn't like being alone.

Nibble is an adventurer who always wears one blue sock. He's extremely curious and loves peanuts.

Abby is a gentle and thoughtful mouse. She is very proud of her long tail but doesn't like her pink nose.

One day the Five Nice Mice saw the most exciting
thing on the Mouse Notice Board: an announcement
for The Great Car Race.
Not only were they thrilled about the idea of a race,
but they could barely contain themselves when they
saw what the Grand Prize would be: the biggest piece
of cheese anyone had ever seen.
It was an opportunity that was too good to
miss, so they sat up the whole night
designing the ultimate race car.

"We'll need a car engine, of course, and the right kind of batteries," said Whisk.

"And a steering wheel," added Nibble.

"We'll need four tires," said Abby, "and a horn. The car has to have a horn!"

"I think it would be nice to have some lights," said Teeny.

"Don't worry about screws and nails," said Bon Bon, "I have lots of those."

The next morning they began their search.

They looked in every imaginable place.

"Look at this colorful tin can," said Nibble.

"Are you thinking what I'm thinking?" asked Whisk. And they all agreed.

"Put it on the cart. It's perfect."

They found other bits and bobs, odds and ends, and even a couple
thingamajigs they were sure would be useful. They didn't stop until
they had collected everything they needed to build the perfect car.

Whisk was good at building things and got right to work.
"Muscle power is my speciality," said Bon Bon,
"let me help you with that."
"The tires are ready to go on," said Abby.

Teeny wanted to know what Nibble was up to.
He was being rather secretive. "What is it…
exactly, you're working on?" she asked.
"For such an important race we must be prepared for
everything. This is a surprise… just in case," he said.

When it was finished, they all admired their creation.
"Our very own race car!" said Whisk proudly.
"Who's going to drive?" asked Abby.
They all looked at each other.
None of the Five Nice Mice
had ever driven a car.

Then they started talking at once about who should and who shouldn't,
and who couldn't possibly, until a loud voice announced, "Stop! I'll drive."
It was Nibble. No one disagreed.

"We need to practice," said Nibble, and so they all got in.

They drove slowly at first, and then
they went faster and faster.
It was, after all, a race car.

They tried zigging and then zagging and were
feeling quite pleased with their little car, when
they heard a powerful motor coming up from behind.
It was a shiny red car, and it easily sped past them.

They had found their competition.

The morning of the race the Five Nice Mice
were so excited. Every mouse in town came
to see it. Each of the cars had a number,
and the drivers were preparing for the start.

"Oh my," said Teeny, her little voice sounding nervous.
"Look at car number four!"
It was none other than the shiny red car that flew past them yesterday.
It was a powerful, radio-controlled model that looked like it had just
come from the toy shop.

"Forget car number four," said Whisk.
"Look at the cheese!"

Then a big, booming voice announced:
"Mice… START... YOUR... ENGINES!"
The starting flag waved, and they were off!

The course took them through a side street
full of people—people with big feet.
Every driver had to concentrate to avoid being stepped
on.

"I'm glad you practiced your zigging and zagging,"
said Bon Bon.
"Look over there at Number 3," said Whisk.
"I think he zigged when he should have zagged!"

"Thank goodness he's okay," said Abby, "but he hit
the wall. I'm afraid he won't be finishing the race."

"The red car is first," said Nibble, "we'd better speed up."

The Five Nice Mice were soon out on the open street.
They went faster and faster, but the red car was
already out of sight.

Just then something else started heading straight
toward them.

"Woof, woof!" barked a deep voice.
"Oh no, a dog!" squeaked Teeny.
"Hurry, please. His paws are bigger
 than our car."
"Turn!" shouted Bon Bon.
"Turn in there."

They zoomed into a tunnel, where they were safe.
But it was dark, and there were noises. Teeny switched
on the headlamp just in time for them to dodge another
mouse in a wind-up car.
"That's it, I've had it!" said Teeny,
"I was almost trampled by big feet, overrun by giant
paws, and nearly crashed into another car.
What's next, I ask you?"
"The dog has gone," said Bon Bon calmly.
"It's okay."

Back in the race,
the Five Nice Mice passed a café.
They had not lost much time and
were now in third place.

They turned into the park, and Nibble stepped
on the accelerator. A park could be a dangerous place.
There were always joggers, dogs, mothers with strollers
and even children!

Just then a giant red ball came flying overhead and bounced right in front of them. They swerved and missed it, but it bounced again, and they swerved again.

"Phew, that was close!" said Whisk.

"Too close," said Nibble. "Let's get out of this silly park."

As soon as they left the park, they saw car number one stopped with smoke pouring out of it.

"We've blown the engine," said one of the mice, disappointed.
"Hurry, you're second now, but there's some rough driving ahead!"

"The outdoor market," said Abby.
"This is the biggest obstacle course yet."
"It smells wonderful," said Teeny.
"I think I smell peanuts," said Nibble.

"Forget peanuts, watch out for the feet!" shouted Whisk.
"And pigeons—look out for the pigeons!"
"Where's the red car?" asked Bon Bon. "I don't see it."
"Could they be that far ahead?" asked Nibble.

"Well, look at that," said Bon Bon. "They've stopped for a little snack."
"I knew I smelled peanuts—sugar-covered peanuts. Hurrah!" said Nibble.
"Hey look," said the driver of the red car, "it's the mice in the silver and
  blue tin car. Let's go!"

The Five Nice Mice jumped back in their car.

Both cars flew past the fountain and sped down a steep slope when Abby shouted, "Slow down, there's a sharp turn at the bottom of this hill!"

Nibble immediately shifted to a lower gear, and the car slowed as the turn approached.

The red car sailed by, but it took the corner too fast and flipped over.

"Fix the wheel and flip the car back over!"
shouted the red car's driver to his team.

Now the Five Nice Mice were in the lead. Abby and Bon Bon
began to cheer, but the engine started to cough, and with
a strange clanking sound, the car began to slow down.
"What's wrong?" cried Teeny.
"It must be the battery," said Whisk.

The red car started up again, and it was getting closer.
"What are we going to do?" asked Abby. "We can't lose now!"

"I think it's time for my surprise," said Nibble.
"But we don't have enough battery power for your plan," said Whisk.
"We have even stronger power," said Nibble. "Hold on tight."
There was a snap and a whoosh, and the secret, just-in-case surprise
popped open.

It was a sail. Now they could travel by wind power.

But would it be enough?
The red car was gaining speed.
It was getting closer.
Soon they were side by side.
Then there was a gust of wind!

The crowd went wild, applauding
and cheering for the two teams.

When they crossed the finish line,
the announcer said,
"Ladies and Gentlemice,
the winners of the Great Car Race
and the Grand Prize...
In car number five...
It's the Five... Nice... Mice!"

The five little mice could hardly
believe they had won.

Once the Ultimate Cheese was loaded onto a cart, the Five Nice Mice headed for home. When they arrived, they turned and saw that all the other mice had followed them.

The winners realized there was only one thing
to do—throw the Ultimate Cheese Party!
Everyone was invited to join them.

And because the Five Nice Mice shared their prize,
everyone felt like a winner.